They continue along a shared path in the forest and learn about one another as they walk. It is remarkable how much they have in common and how close they become. They discover the parallel depths of their wounds and the corresponding reaches of their endurance. Together they find a clearing and build a home. Love is with them. He teaches her how to find the light and create a household. She teaches him how to dance and laugh and sing and play. They hold each other with cherished gratitude.

For many years the land and the love bring them more joy than either had ever known. However, togetherness also brings them hardship. The one who can't allow himself to be afraid feels threatened by the one who must let her fear be known. The one who must let her fear be known feels threatened by the one who can't allow himself to be afraid. They have no understanding of this.

One day, the fearful one is trying to find a trail but takes a wrong turn. She is lost in the darkness again. When she finally makes her way home, she needs soothing for her fear—but instead her fear brings discomfort to her soulmate. Now the darkness has entered their home. She asks him if they can try going to the sea, for it is open to the sky and the light. He isn't sure he can face its vast, unenclosed expanse and even ponders leaving for the mountains instead, but she convinces him to join her.

They find a small boat and enter the water. Before they can turn back, the sky begins to blacken. Thick clouds overspread the atmosphere. The sea is raging. She can't contain her fright. He cannot explain why but knows he is unable to be with her fear, and he feels he must leave the boat. As the boat gets tossed, he sees a reef resembling a mountain ridge and tells her he wants to swim out to it and stay there on his own. She is concerned for his safety, and she can't fathom why he won't stay in the boat with her. His need to leave hurts her deeply. She doesn't want to be left alone in such treacherous waters, perhaps never to see him again, but she is overwhelmed with doubt and confusion. As the winds howl and the ocean roars, she can't comprehend what is happening. She makes sure his life jacket is firmly fastened, gives him her love, and lets him go. He thanks her and tells her he loves her—that he always will—and begins to swim away. She doesn't understand. She did not know then what she would someday grasp: that he couldn't understand either...and that he never left her.

She is alone now. She had brought her beloved away from the forest to the sea, and now he is off to somewhere strange and distant. She didn't hold onto him. She let him go. She is lost in the storm. The boat hurtles into a cave that holds a scream which echoes back and forth for eternity. It sounds like hers. When she asks its meaning, it only echoes back her questions. She screams; the echo renews its reverberation. She tries to decipher its message, but encounters only echoes of her questions and her screams.

She stays alone in the cave waiting for the storm to abate while the waves crash against its outer walls. She calls out to her lost soulmate, wondering if he can hear her. Her cries swirl around in the echo. The wind blows through her. Suddenly—in it, she hears her soulmate's voice. It goes to her heart. She weeps. She hears it again. This time it seems to be calling out for the light. She fears he is in danger. She longs to be by his side, but they are both lost in this storm. She sends her love to him through the ocean's current, asking if they can please be together, and hopes it reaches him. A ripple reaches back to her with his weakened voice saying he loves her and wants to be with her.

The next day, she roams bewildered in an unfamiliar, deserted place. She's haunted by an echo which won't go away and by images of a devastating storm. Was it real? Where is she? What is this place? Has she washed ashore? What has happened? The blinding light reveals to her that the storm has ended, but that it has taken her soulmate with it. She wasn't with him. He was alone and afraid. Last night he was in her heart. Today her heart feels as though it has been torn from her. In agony she screams, but the scream has no sound. She tries again, but it remains silent. Although the scream can't be heard, its anguish permeates her spirit and is deafening.

She reaches out to hold her soulmate, but he is not there. She searches for him to no avail. It is too late. Has she caused this? She wishes with all her might that she had held onto him in the boat as tightly as she could...and that she had not asked him to take this journey. She writhes on the ground in grief. She tries to remember their life together in the forest, but memories of the stormy sea flood over it. The forest seems so far away, never to be found again. It hurts too much to remember the forest, with its abundant life and love, when she is now in this desolate place without sustenance and without love. She reaches into thin air, into nothingness. It is unclear how one would survive here. The boat is gone. There doesn't appear to be any way out.

With all the strength she can muster, she desperately tries to yell for help. Mercifully, the wind can detect her distress and summons a kind fisherman to row out to her. The fisherman finds her and lifts her frail body onto his dory. He wants to learn how she became stranded in this forsaken place, and he listens with compassionate wisdom. He offers to guide her to safety. The sea is his home, and he knows it as he knows his heart. He shows her that the ocean can bring peace, as she had once hoped it could. She wishes this fisherman had been met before the storm; it must have been her soulmate, she believes, who instructed the wind to bring the fisherman to her now.

As they row, the fisherman sings. She remembers singing with her beloved. How she aches for him and their life together. Memories of the storm shake her. The fisherman tries to comfort her by explaining that the storm's gripping force and disturbing chaos may stay with her for ages, and this is no fault of her own. That is why it is important to sing—so the turbulence can be soothed. She aspires to learn and understand. Although her heart is heavy, she tries to join in the song. When he delivers her back to land, he promises to watch over her always.

She walks upon unfamiliar ground with sea legs. How strange to be back on land without her soulmate. Tears stream down her cheeks as sorrow engulfs her. Memories of the storm flash before her again, striking her with deep regret. She remembers the fisherman's lesson and begins to sing. Each day alone she tries to sing. Years pass, and still she sings. One day, unexpectedly, she hears the same song being sung. She seeks its source and finds an old man who is also alone. They sing together; the song resonates throughout the terrain. The birds chime in until the sound fills the sky and rays of sunshine dance to its melody. She and the old man are profoundly grateful to have found life again. Love fully fills their hearts. They both know its precious meaning. Thus they treasure, nurture, protect, and hold it tenderly. They rejoice.

Together they go to the shore for enjoyment. She must help the old man traverse the sand and carry him over the rocks. Their love is so sure that she doesn't mind caring for him nor does he mind that she must do so. No matter how strenuous the challenges become, they do not stop their visits to the shore. The old man grows weaker. Oh, she cannot bear to lose him. She fears for the day when she will again be alone. The storm still seizes her memory and thrashes at her heart. But, nonetheless, she fully sings her song with the old man.

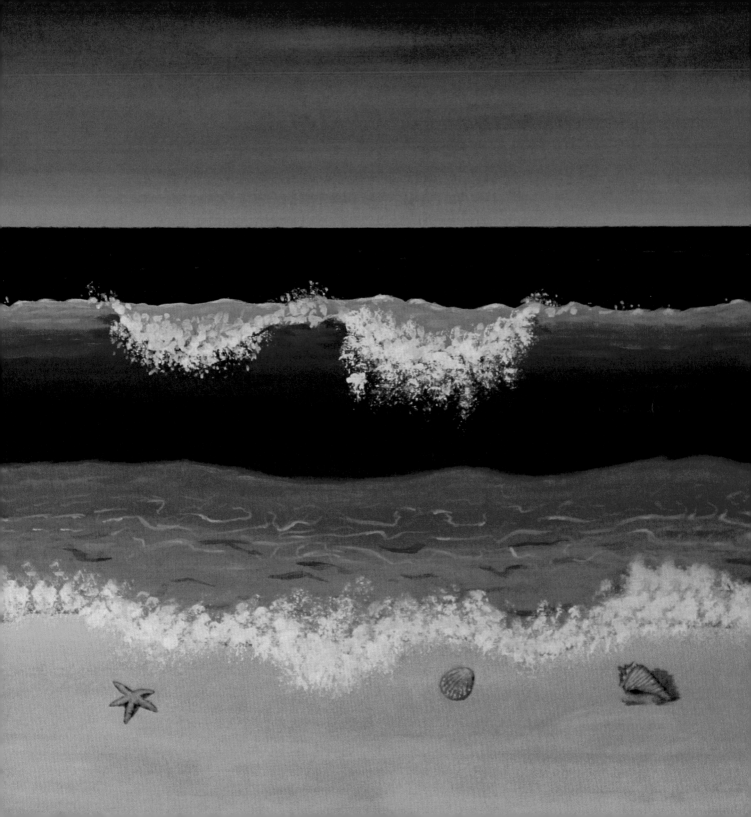

One day, they head to the old man's most special place—the lighthouse. He relies upon her to lift him the entire way. She uses every ounce of her strength to bring him to their destination. He seems to be at peace there. They hold hands in loving gratitude as they watch the tide rise. Just at that moment, a wave washes over them and takes them away with it. As the wave recedes, they are still hand in hand—but the old man is no longer breathing. He has passed.

She falls to her knees and weeps as the sun sets on the horizon. Both her soulmates have been taken by the sea. That ruinous storm has never left her, and now it feels closer in intensity because of this loss. She doesn't scream this time, though. She begins to realize that the journey to the sea was in search of healing, and the storm was beyond her control. She was not the cause. The fear that once overpowered her has somehow become an accepted part of her. She can open herself to mourning.

Soon darkness falls. In the beacon from the lighthouse a form can be seen. It is the fisherman rowing towards her. His song can be heard harmonizing with the night sky. He gently approaches her. He explains that he knows she is not able to sing now, but when the time comes that she can sing again, she will hear her soulmates singing with her. She will recognize the storm, the calm, the love, the loss, and the wholeness of life in her song. It will be the song that echoes inside her instead of the scream. The song will connect her to the wholeness so she will not feel alone.

The fisherman delicately places her in his boat. This time he will take her

to the forest. She is ready to see it now.

The author had a tragedy occur as an adolescent and lost most of her tongue. To be able to sing is a miracle to her!

She had two loving partners who died—Leon Wisel and Benjamin Harsip. She now shares life with her dear partner—Patty Correia.

Her work with bereavement counselor Judy Seifert, trauma specialist Sandra Phinney, and physician Harvey Zarren has brought her the healing of _An Essential Song_.

Made in the USA
Lexington, KY
17 February 2018